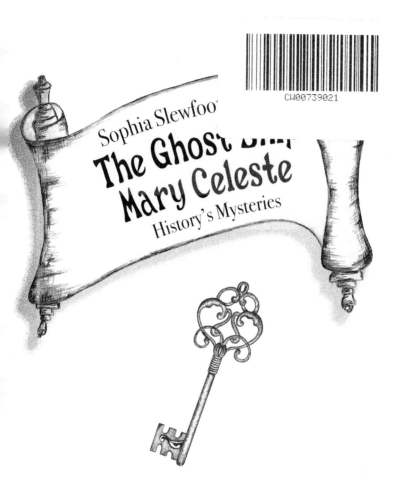

Sophia Slewfoot

The Ghost Ship Mary Celeste

History's Mysteries

Marie-Louise Gregory

Illustrated by Nicola Brooks

A CIP catalogue record for this title is available from the
British Library.

ISBN 978-1-7398655-0-4 (Paperback)

2 4 6 8 10 9 7 5 3 1

First published 2021

Muddy Publishing Ltd
www.muddypublishing.com

Dedications

To my real life Sophia and all the little heroines
and heroes like her. Read, learn and see where your
imagination takes you.

Chapter 1

Sophia Slewfoot was an ordinary ten year old girl, but today was not an ordinary day.

After school she would be moving house and that was uppermost in Sophia's thoughts all day. Even during her favourite lesson, history, Sophia could not concentrate. Sophia's mind was spinning, round and round like a carousel at the fair; and her tummy felt like it was flipping and churning, as if a roller-coaster was rushing around inside her. Was she excited? Was she nervous? Would she be happy in the new house or would she miss her lovely, old home? All she could think about was what her new house would be like.

In the run-up to moving day, Sophia had heard her mum and dad telling their friends and family that the house was "a bit of a project" and "a doer-upper". Sophia didn't know what that meant, exactly, but she knew that the house would need quite a lot of work before it would be as warm, comfortable and homely as the one she had left that morning. In fact, Sophia was picturing a dark, dingy, even derelict, tumbledown house and she was actually very much dreading the end of the school day.

When the bell finally rang for home-time, Sophia did not want to move, but her best friend, Betty Babbington, yanked her to her feet.

"Come on Sophs!" said Betty. "You never know, moving house might be the start of a great adventure!"

Reluctantly, Sophia started to gather together her bag, coat, water bottle, PE kit, art work, reading book, lunch box and all the other gubbins that school kids seem to lug around on a daily basis.

"All right then Bets," she sighed. "I suppose I'm only delaying the inevitable. Ok, I'll head 'home' then."

Sophia and Betty walked out of school and down the path to the school gate. Since they had turned ten, Sophia, Betty and some of the other children in their class had been allowed to walk home without their parents. Until now, that had felt grown-up and exciting, but that was perhaps because Sophia and Betty had lived so close to each other, just down the road from their school on the edge of the village. Today, for the first time, however, instead of merrily chatting and laughing her way down the street with her friend, Sophia was going to have to leave school and walk in the opposite direction, towards the centre of the village and to the 'unknown' that she would, from now, have to call 'home'.

Sophia was, in the main, a very happy and outgoing girl. She was short and slight for her age, but she was very sporty and loved dancing, running and horse-riding and played tennis and football every week. Sophia had crazy, curly blond hair which she studiously tried to tame into a plait or a ponytail every day, but which inevitably escaped its bobble after approximately five minutes, making her look constantly tousled, even a little bit bedraggled, no matter how hard she tried! She loved her family and her pet Beagle, Toby, and, along with Betty, she had a great group of girlfriends who were always giggling and gossiping about something. When she felt unsure about something, though, or when she went somewhere new, or met someone for the first time, she could be quite quiet – sometimes even shy. She was, deep down, a thoughtful and sensitive little girl. Perhaps that was why she got on so well with Betty. Betty was tall, strong and a few months older than Sophia. She had long shining, straight blonde hair and she was a confident, clever and kindly girl who was pretty-much fearless. Together, one cautious and one carefree, they made a great team.

Betty gave Sophia a big squeeze at the school gate.

"Go on Sophs! I bet the new house will feel like home before you know it, and you'll have loads of fun exploring in the meantime. Have a happy moving day – and radio me later to tell me all about it!"

Feeling energised by Betty's excitement, and now actually 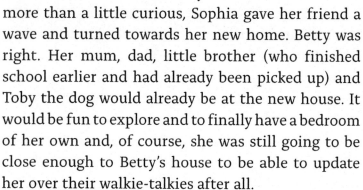 more than a little curious, Sophia gave her friend a wave and turned towards her new home. Betty was right. Her mum, dad, little brother (who finished school earlier and had already been picked up) and Toby the dog would already be at the new house. It would be fun to explore and to finally have a bedroom of her own and, of course, she was still going to be close enough to Betty's house to be able to update her over their walkie-talkies after all.

Chapter 2

As Sophia walked home, all she thought about was the new house. Her mum and dad had shown her pictures of it in a brochure and she had seen photos from when her mum and dad had looked around, but she still couldn't imagine actually living there. She had loved the cosy little cottage that her family had lived in ever since she was a baby. The closer she got to the village centre, the more her stomach started to flip-flop again, and her feelings of uncertainty and anxiety began to return. Suddenly, the house came into view. Sophia realised that the move was really happening, and she started to tremble inside. A minute later she was standing at the front door – her hand shaking slightly as she turned the handle.

Inside, Sophia saw removal men everywhere – lifting boxes, shifting the family's old furniture and moving everything into its new place. The house was a hive of activity. The removal men were all moving quickly and carefully, each with a different job to do. Sophia was reminded of worker bees, busily buzzing around flowers, collecting pollen and working together as a team, and she understood why that phrase was so apt.

The second Sophia walked through the door, she saw Toby bounding towards her with his tail wagging and his tongue hanging out as he smiled, panting happily, to greet her. She saw her little brother, surrounded by empty boxes and toys all over the floor, already playing with his Lego; her dad making cups of tea and chatting with (distracting!) the moving men; and her mum frantically cleaning, unpacking and loudly directing all traffic.

'Hmm' thought Sophia 'maybe things won't be so different here after all!'

Sophia shook off her concerns and strode confidently in to the new house. She dropped all her bags and other paraphernalia and gave Toby a stroke. He jumped up in delight. He too had found the impending move a little disturbing over the last few days, as he could always sense when Sophia was feeling unnerved. Now, though, he was clearly over the moon to have all the family together, cheerfully settling in. After a lovely cuddle with Toby, a passing nod from her brother, a high five from her dad and a hurried but heartfelt hug from her mum, Sophia started to explore her new home.

Her parents had been right. The house was going

to be a project. In a lesson last year, when Sophia had learned all about the history of the village, she had discovered that this house was nearly three hundred years old. As she wandered round, she could see that, at one time, the house may have been quite grand, but in recent years it had been left empty and uncared for. Faded wallpaper was peeling off the walls, bare floorboards creaked uneasily underfoot, and there were ominous, damp, mouldy patches in some of the dark and dusty corners of long-unused rooms.

Now that she was here, though, Sophia didn't feel scared or worried at all. Rather, she was excited and eager to explore all of the nooks and crannies of this big, old house and to discover what secrets it might hold. Sophia's favourite subject at school was history. She loved learning about what people's lives had been like at different times in the past, and she was fascinated by some of the stories she had heard in her lessons: murder, mystery, royal feuds, pirates, power-struggles... Honestly, you couldn't make up some of the things that had actually happened – in real life! – through the mists of time.

One of the reasons for the move had been so that Sophia could have a bedroom of her very own. She was looking forward to no longer having to share a room with her funny but noisy and messy little brother. Keen to see her new bedroom, Sophia made her way up the creaking staircase and along the landing, with its once luxurious, but now threadbare, carpet. As she did so, with Toby trotting by her side, busily sniffing and snuffling all the while, she glanced into her parents' new bedroom, her brother's room and a large storage cupboard.

Just before she reached her own room, Sophia noticed that Toby had become especially interested in a patch of ill-fitting skirting board running along the bottom of the landing wall. He had started sniffing quite frantically, and then began pawing and scratching at the skirting and the base of the wall, in an almost agitated fashion. Sophia had never seen Toby acting in such a manner before, and so she decided to take a closer look.

With her nose wrinkled somewhat (in anticipation of discovering that it was a big hairy spider or some other creepy crawly, or perhaps a particularly smelly patch of mouldy plaster or rotten wood, that was bothering Toby), Sophia knelt down on the dusty, well-worn carpet. She peered closely at the skirting board and the wall above it. Sophia was surprised to see that, in fact, the skirting was crudely attached, not to the solid landing wall as she had thought, but to an almost-concealed panel. The panel, which was quite small, had no frame and was built into the wall and papered. It formed part of the wall itself and was almost entirely hidden from view.

Sophia had heard from her mum and dad that the new house had enough bedrooms for her and her brother to have their own, but she hadn't heard that there would be a spare. Thinking that the panel must be the door to another, smaller, storage cupboard, Sophia pushed on it gently. Sophia was amazed to discover that it was indeed a door that popped open, but that it was not the door to a storage cupboard or even to an unexpected spare bedroom. In fact, the door led to another staircase – a very tight, winding staircase that spiralled upwards towards the roof of the house.

Sophia was intrigued! Just like a Beagle on the scent of a bone, Sophia could sense adventure! Where did the staircase lead? What could be up there? She couldn't wait to find out, but before she and Toby could explore any further, she heard her dad call "Come on kids! Moving day takeaway for tea!"

Chapter 3

After a treat tea of pizza and pop, Sophia couldn't wait to run up to her new bedroom – a room of her very own at last! Apart from wanting to get settled in and to feel at home before her first bedtime in the new house, Sophia wanted to unpack some of her essentials, and to radio Betty with the update. She raced upstairs as fast as she could.

In her new bedroom, Sophia looked around happily and began to unpack. The first box that she tackled contained all Toby's toys, chews and of course his fleecy blankets and dog bed. As soon as Sophia laid Toby's bed down in a cosy spot at the end of her bed, he dived into it, rolled and curled himself around until he was as snug as a bug in a rug having a hug, and almost immediately started snoring contentedly. It was clear to Sophia that Toby had already decided that he did not mind where he was at all, as long as he was with her.

Next Sophia started to unpack her own things. Once she had tidied away all her own toys and carefully positioned her teddies, her cushions, her snuggle blanket and her precious Cloth Rabbit (her sleeping companion since she had been a tiny baby) on her bed, Sophia grabbed her 'go-bag' and got comfy, ready for her moving day de-brief with Betty.

Sophia and Betty both had go-bags. Being great fans of mystery stories and whodunnit books, they were both very keen amateur detectives. They spent a lot of their spare time learning about, and honing, their sleuthing skills. In particular, they were well aware that a good detective must be ready for adventure and action at a moment's notice, and so Sophia and Betty had each assembled rucksacks full of essential kit. As well as:

- notebooks
- pens (several, because a detective can't afford for his or her pen to run out just when vital notes need taking)
- a torch (with spare batteries – allowing a torch to die just when you needed it most was, they knew, a real rookie error)
- binoculars

- sunglasses and a selection of hats (for when the need for a swift disguise arises)
- a paperback detective novel (for inspiration and for passing the time on stakeouts)
- a purse containing a few pounds (for emergencies)
- snacks (for energy and because, well, there's always room for snacks) and
- a magnifying glass (obviously)

Sophia's and Betty's go-bags contained one each of a pair of military grade (almost) walkie-talkies, which Sophia had bought with all of her Christmas and birthday money added together. The walkie-talkies were primarily for enabling Sophia and Betty to communicate when they were out and about solving mysteries, shadowing suspects and pursuing separate lines of enquiry on active investigations. However they also came in very handy for when the best friends liked to chat to each other but were not allowed to borrow and hog their parents' mobile phones. It was the walkie-talkie that Sophia grabbed now.

"Betty, Betty – come in Betty!" Sophia didn't have

to wait a minute before her walkie-talkie crackled into life and Betty replied.

"I'm here Sophs! How's it going?! How's the new house?!"

"Oh Betty, it's brilliant!" Sophia cried excitedly. "I don't know what I was so worried about before. Toby is right at home already and I don't have to share a room with Ted anymore! Best of all, though, I've got the feeling that the house might hold some mysteries for us to solve, or some adventures for us to unravel. I've only been here for about five minutes and I've already found a hidden door which seems to lead to a secret staircase...!"

"Roger that Sophs!" laughed Betty, immediately thrilled at the thought of a real life Enid Blyton-like investigation. "It's Saturday tomorrow – I'll be round at yours, reporting for duty, straight after breakfast!"

After a bit more chat and a lot more giggles, the two girls rang off their walkie-talkie radios. Sophia changed into her pjs, brushed her teeth and clambered into bed. Toby stirred and, although he wasn't strictly supposed to, he jumped up onto Sophia's bed and laid his head on her lap as she read a few chapters from her Ultimate Detective's Handbook. Before she knew it, Sophia was drifting off to sleep and dreaming about best friends, secret doors, hidden passages, exploration and investigation...

Chapter 4

Sophia woke up bright and early on Saturday morning and smiled to herself as she realised that she already felt perfectly at home in her new room and the new house. Toby was snoring peacefully next to her and she could hear her little brother enacting a battle to the death between his Lego Batman and Joker in his room next door – just like every other morning since he had discovered (a) Lego and (b) superheroes.

The only thing to dampen her mood was when Betty's mum called, just after breakfast, to say that Betty couldn't come over after all. Her grandma was unwell and Betty's family were travelling over to take care of her at her remote but beautiful old cottage on the North Wales island of Anglesey. Betty's family would be away all weekend and, although Sophia would miss having her around, she knew that Betty would be happy to visit, and to help look after, her gran.

Not to be deterred, Sophia excused herself from the slightly less frenzied now, but nevertheless still quite chaotic, cleaning and unpacking that her parents were undertaking all around the house. After setting

Ted up with a new Lego set that would hopefully keep him quiet for a good couple of hours, Sophia turned her attention (at last!) to the hidden doorway and the secret staircase.

With her go-bag on her back, Sophia pressed lightly on the wallpapered door. She held up her torch and peered cautiously at the dark, dusty staircase that spiralled up ahead of her. Taking a deep breath, feeling a shiver down her spine, and with her faithful Tobes at her side (of course), Sophia crept gingerly through the door. With butterflies in her stomach from both anxiety and excitement, Sophia began to slowly and carefully climb the steep, narrow stairs.

With one hand holding up the torch and the other sweeping away the creepy cobwebs that hung and clung across the bare brick walls of the winding staircase, Sophia's progress was slow. She also realised, after several steps, that she was holding her breath, as if she unconsciously felt the need to proceed absolutely silently. Telling herself that that was silly – she was in her own house after all! – Sophia allowed herself to take a few bracing breaths, before finding herself at the top of the stairs and in a small, circular space that was almost too small to be described as a room.

The tiny, round room was completely empty. Sophia felt not just a little disappointed. Surely her adventure couldn't be over already, pretty much before it had even begun? But, after just a minute or so, her detective's intuition kicked in and she realised that surely no one would go to the trouble of constructing a space like this, accessed via a secret staircase and a hidden door, for no reason at all. Perhaps it was one of those priest holes that she had learned about in her history lessons, where priests and other religious practitioners had hidden away and taken refuge from first Henry VIII's and then Mary I's and Elizabeth I's henchmen? But no, this house dated back to the 1700s, a good few hundred years ago, but not as far back as Tudor times.

So what could such a space have been used for? Why would anyone construct a secret door, stairs and room... unless the reason was to hide something that was meant to remain undiscovered?

Seizing on that as a working theory, Sophia put her sleuthing skills to work immediately. Remembering how the Famous Five had discovered many-a secret passageway and hidey-hole through probing and pressing walls and seeking out false panels, Sophia began to systematically scrutinise the old, rounded, crumbling, bare brick walls.

And suddenly there it was... a safe! Built into the wall, at about Sophia's head height, was an ancient metal safe. It had rusted so much that it was now an orangey red colour, which meant that it was almost entirely camouflaged in the old red brick room. Sophia was overjoyed to have made such an intriguing discovery! She soon found, though, that, of course, the safe was locked, fast.

Chapter 5

Sophia had already come so far. She had found a hidden doorway and a secret staircase. She had braved the dark and the dusty cobwebs and had climbed the spiral stairs to find a hidden hidey-hole room. In that room, she had deployed searching skills worthy of the Famous Five and had located an ancient safe. So, undeterred, like all good sleuths, Sophia decided to investigate thoroughly before even considering giving up in the face of a rusty old lock.

Sophia was desperately curious to find out what was inside the safe. It must be something really, really special for someone to have gone to all these lengths to keep it secret and secure. Sophia was incredibly excited to have found a real life mystery here, in her very own new home, and so it didn't occur to her at all that someone may have gone to such lengths, not to protect whatever was inside the safe, but perhaps to keep outsiders safe from it...?

One way or another, though, Sophia knew that she had to work out how to open the safe. She thought of the huge bunch of keys that her parents had been given when they moved into the house, but quickly dismissed the idea that the key to an ancient hidden safe would have been casually handed over by the estate agent alongside keys to the house, the garage and the ramshackle old shed at the bottom of the garden! No, she felt quite sure that if someone had gone to the trouble of constructing a hidden staircase leading to a secret room and then installing an ancient safe, they must also have gone to some effort to hide the key.

Hmm, but where? How on earth could Sophia suddenly sniff out an old safe key that had probably lain hidden away in some unknown, secret nook for years and years and years? It could be, well, it could be anywhere! But, wait a minute! 'Sniff out'... that was it! In a flash of deductive genius, Sophia realised that she had, at her disposal, one of the most effective tools possible for locating something... Toby! Tobes was a Beagle and they were famed for their ability to seize upon, and then track, a scent. As Toby was one of the best sniffer dogs in the business, all Sophia would have to do would be to set him on the scent of the missing safe key, and then wait for him to follow his nose!

Toby was, as per usual, snuffling and snuggling at his beloved mistress' feet, so Sophia simply scooped him up and let him have a serious sniff around the safe and, in particular, the lock. Almost immediately, Toby's ears pricked up in excitement. He started pawing gently at Sophia to let her know that he had cottoned on to a scent and wanted to get down on to the floor to follow it!

Sophia didn't have to wait long! After just a few minutes of Toby conscientiously and systematically sniffing his way around the tiny, circular space, the little dog stopped short, right in the centre of the room. He began scratching furiously at what appeared to Sophia to be just another dusty floorboard exactly like all the other dusty floorboards in the room. However, it was, of course, not just another floorboard exactly like all the others. Upon closer inspection, when Sophia had blown and brushed away the filmy layer of dust and dirt which covered this hitherto untouched-for-decades floor, it was clear that the floorboard was marked, right in the middle, with a faint, tiny, etched cross. Sophia gasped!

"'X' marks the spot, eh, Tobes?!" she said, grinning

widely and with her eyes shining. Either side of the 'x' were two very small, round holes – each just about big enough for a person to insert their fingertips.

Slightly recoiling at the thought of the webs and bugs that might brush at her fingers from beneath the board, but bravely pressing ahead in any event, Sophia put her thumb and forefinger slowly and carefully into the two small holes, and lifted...

Her hunch had been right! 'X' did indeed mark the spot! As Sophia gently pulled up the old floorboard, she saw that, squirreled away just underneath it, and wrapped in a scrap of musty, fusty, old cloth, was a heavy, metallic and slightly rusting old key. It was by far the most elaborate and ornately crafted key that she had ever seen. It definitely looked like the key to something very special, and she knew at once that it was the one.

Trembling with excitement, and almost breathless at the thought of what treasure or valuable antiques might be revealed when she opened the safe, Sophia turned back to the ancient safe and placed the key into the lock.

The key slid in easily, and turned smoothly within the workings of the lock until, with a satisfying click, the door of the safe swung open!

Shaking with exhilaration and trepidation in equal measure, Sophia held up her torch with one hand, and reached into the safe with the other. She found, both to her delight and bewilderment, an object like nothing she had ever seen before.

Chapter 6

How to describe the curious object that Sophia had found in the old safe in the secret, hidey-hole room?!

Well, at first glance the object looked like an antique clock. It resembled an old-fashioned carriage clock and looked like something that could have held pride of place on a grand Victorian mantelpiece. It was made of what must have been real gold, as the object had surely been locked away for many years, but it was shiny and beautiful and not tarnished at all. The 'clock' face was made of a creamy, shimmering mother-of-pearl, which seemed to glow, even in the tiny, windowless room, just by the faint light of Sophia's torch. Sophia could make out, running around the edge of the face, in Roman numerals fashioned from onyx (a black precious stone), the numbers 1 to 12, just like you would find on an ordinary clock. That, though, was where the similarities to a clock came to an end.

Running around the circular rim of the object, outside the mother-of-pearl face, and etched into the gold itself, were inscriptions which Sophia recognised as corresponding to different periods in history. The periods started, at the top of the object, with 'Pre-history', and ran all the way around (in the clockwise direction), through 3000 BC – 476 AD, 477 AD – 1066, 1066 – 1485, 1486 – 1601, 1602 – 1715, 1716 – 1836, 1837 – 1901, 1902 – 1945, to 1946 – 2021. After 1946 – 2021, for the last few degrees of the circle, there was an almost-blank space, marked only with the notation '?'.

On the mother-of-pearl face, immediately inside the Roman numerals, at the top, bottom and on either side, were the letters N, E, S and W, which Sophia took to stand for north, east, south and west, as on a compass. Then, just inside the compass letters, running clockwise in a circle from the top, were the notations 90°, 60°, 30°, 0°, 30°, 60°; and then 90°, 60°, 30°, 0°, 30° and 60° again. Sophia could make neither head nor tail of the notations, but grabbed a notebook and pen from her go-bag and carefully copied them down. Perhaps the meaning of the notations would be something that she could work out later.

Finally on the mother-of-pearl face, Sophia noticed a faint, thin line which had been scored delicately across from IX (number 9) on the left-hand side, to III (number 3) on the right, and which therefore effectively divided the face into a top half and a bottom half. A few millimetres above the line, in the centre, was the word 'Day', and a few millimetres below the line was the word 'Night'. An arrow-shaped, black, metal 'hand' was affixed to the face, right in the centre, and currently pointed straight up to 'Day'.

Also attached to the face, Sophia noticed, were

several other hands. All of the hands were arrow-shaped, so that they could clearly point to a number, letter, notation or word, but nevertheless the hands were all different. Some were silvery, some gold, some coppery in colour. Some were shiny, some were dull. Some were plain and some were ornately carved. The various different designs made it easy to see that the different hands each related to a different set of inscriptions or notations. There were a big and little hand that seemed to indicate the time via the Roman numerals, as on a normal clock. One hand pointed steadfastly to N and another spun around to indicate direction via the letters whenever Sophia moved the object, so that, together, they operated as if the object was a compass. Another, quite large, hand pointed to a time period. Finally, another pair of hands (again, one big and one little) pointed to the circle of numbers that Sophia had noted down and would investigate later.

Sophia stared, in wonder, at this extraordinary object. She realised that, as well as pointing to Day, the various clock hands were currently pointing to the very end of the 1946 – 2021 time period; to just before 60° in between N and E, and just after 0° next to W ; and to – what? – 10 o'clock? That was strange. Sophia had had a later breakfast than usual because it was the weekend, but she had nevertheless hurried to commence her investigations. She knew that she had rushed up to the hidey-hole room shortly before 10 o'clock in the morning. Sophia felt sure that she had been exploring the staircase and the room, locating the safe and finding and trying the key, and then examining the extraordinary clock-like object for at least a couple of hours (and a rumble in her tummy would seem to suggest that it was definitely past lunchtime!). However, if the clock was right, it seemed as if no time had passed at all.

Suddenly feeling the need for some fresh air and possibly a sandwich or a snack, Sophia decided to put the object back into the safe and to head back downstairs. Before she did so, however, like any good detective would do, Sophia made a quick sketch of the object in one of her notebooks, and was careful to jot down exactly the numbers and notations indicated by the various hands: Day; 2021; just before 60° in between N and E; just after 0° next to W ; and 10 o'clock. Then, carrying her go-bag and torch, and with Toby trotting along at her heels, Sophia wound her way back down the secret staircase and out on to the landing of her new home. She carefully closed the door behind her so that it seemed to disappear into the wall again, and made her way to the kitchen.

When Sophia walked into the kitchen and asked her mum whether it was time yet for lunch she was shocked indeed when her mum replied "Lunchtime Sophs?! You've only just had your breakfast!"

Realising that she'd have to be satisfied with a small snack bar or a piece of fruit, Sophia checked the kitchen clock and, just to be sure, the clock on the cooker too. Her mum and the strange clock/object in the secret room upstairs were right. It was only two minutes past 10 o'clock in the morning. It slowly dawned on Sophia that, for all the time that she had been in the hidden hidey-hole room, time outside – in the rest of the house and the rest of the world – had stood still...

Chapter 7

After her adventure in the secret room at the top of her new home, and after the shock of realising that some magical or mysterious force had made time stand still all the while, Sophia felt in need of a change of scene.

The sun was out, she had a new garden to explore and Toby could do with a walk, so Sophia spent the rest of the day playing with Toby and her little brother Ted.

First they explored the new garden. It was large, overgrown and unkempt, and it felt to the children like a wonderful wilderness, full of places to play and hide. Ted's imagination was already running away with him, and before long he was forging through old, gnarled and knotted trees, bushes and undergrowth with his toy sword, anticipating dragons to slay or princesses to rescue around each and every corner. After an hour or two, Sophia and Ted had a quick kick-about with the football, and enjoyed a garden-picnic lunch. Later on, they spent a lovely afternoon scampering along the towpath which ran alongside the canal that by-passed the village, so that Toby could have a good sniff around and they could all really stretch their legs.

So it wasn't until much later, after the family had finished their first proper evening meal together in the new house, that Sophia turned her thoughts again to the curious artefact that she had discovered earlier that day.

Sophia went up to her room soon after tea on the pretext of needing an early night after a busy day and lots of fresh air. She decided that she would do as the funny but brilliant Belgian detective Hercule Poirot often did, and use her 'little grey cells' (that is, her brain power) to solve the mystery of what the object actually was.

Sophia snuggled up on her bed with Toby and settled in to some serious rumination. Obviously, she thought, the object had something to do with time. For the whole, say, two to three hour period that Sophia had been exploring the hidey-hole room and discovering and examining the object, time elsewhere, and to everyone else, had stood still. It was also clear that the object was – in part at least – an actual clock which told the time. In addition, Sophia was able to deduce, from the fact that one of the levels of notation on the object's face began with the words "Pre-history", and included notations such as "BC" and "AD", that the object was also somehow concerned with different time periods throughout history.

Consulting the notes that she had made before she had returned the object to the safe, and concentrating hard, Sophia quickly made a crucial connection. All of the hands relating to time and date had corresponded exactly with the actual time and date that morning: it was daytime, 10 o'clock in the morning and in the year 2021. Following that line of thought and applying it to the other hands and notations, which seemed to resemble a compass and could therefore potentially relate to direction or position, Sophia made what would turn out to be an inspired deduction. She asked herself: could the object also relate to place? Looking at her notes again, Sophia wondered. Could "just before 60° in between N and E and just after 0° next to W" be co-ordinates of some kind, and therefore indicating location?

Sophia knew that her little grey cells could take her only so far. She would now need to deploy another device from any good detective's arsenal: research.

Sophia and Ted shared a tablet, which they used for school work and homework, which was often set online, and for watching kids' TV on Saturday and Sunday mornings when their mum and dad wanted a lie-in. That was what Sophia needed now. Ordinarily neither Sophia nor Ted were allowed the tablet in their bedroom. However, luckily for Sophia, in all the excitement of moving, the tablet had not yet been unpacked and was still in a box at the bottom of her bed.

Sophia grabbed her tablet. "Hmm, what on earth should I actually research, Tobes?" she asked out loud. Toby cocked his head to one side and looked deep in thought for a moment, but unfortunately was unable to offer any helpful advice. On a hunch, therefore, and applying the logic that if the object's date and time information corresponded to reality then its location information might too, Sophia tapped into the internet search engine the name of her village, followed simply by the word "coordinates".

Sophia had made a brilliant breakthrough. The first hit read "Lat. 53.3817 N, Long. 2.4800 W. "Of course!" Sophia cried excitedly to Toby. "The remaining hands refer to latitude and longitude – coordinates by which the location of anywhere on earth can be plotted. The hands on the object pointed to just before 60° in between N and E and just after 0° next to W and we now know that those are the latitude and longitude coordinates for right here in the village!"

Sophia felt hugely pleased with herself for figuring out what all of the notations on the object referred to. It was getting late and it had been an incredibly exciting day. Sophia was just getting ready to drift off into a satisfied sleep, when an arresting thought made her sit bolt upright in bed...

If the object could command time (it had, of course, seemed that the object had made time stand still that morning), could it also determine place? Could time and space be altered and dictated by the moving and setting of the object's various hands? Was the object, in fact, a time machine; or even more than that... was it actually a machine that could enable travel through time and place?!

Sophia's mind boggled. With the prospect of peacefully drifting off to sleep now long gone, Sophia allowed Toby to jump up on to her bed and to nestle in against her while she questioned, over and over again in her mind, whether the object she had discovered might actually be a time- and place-travel machine. As she lay in bed, unable to sleep for excitement, she plotted a daring experiment to find out.

Chapter 8

It was all Sophia could do to contain herself through breakfast the next morning. It was a Sunday, so her mum and dad had had a lie-in. With Batman having been victorious in his battle against Joker the day before, Ted had spent the early morning busily building an impressive Arkham Asylum to imprison the quirky villain. Sophia had therefore been able to take the opportunity to do some pre-breakfast research on antique time machines and navigational devices.

She had learned about something called a sextant, with which mariners from ancient times right up to the modern day had navigated the globe on voyages of exploration and discovery. Sextants measured the angles between the horizon and the stars to work out latitude, longitude, and therefore location. She came across a strange artefact called an astrolabe, which used the sun, stars, the horizon and the meridian for timekeeping, surveying, geography

Sextant

Astrolabe

and astrology. She also discovered something called a planisphere, which was effectively a multi-layered star chart, dating back to the second century, which could be used for calculating the display of visible stars and constellations in the night sky at any time and date.

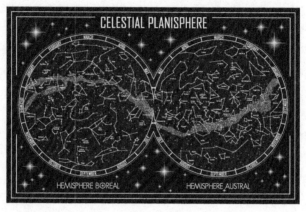

Planisphere

Sophia had decided that, if she was right that the object she had discovered in the old safe in the hidden hidey-hole room at the top of her new (but actually very old) house was a time and space machine, she was going to call it a planisphera-temporalabe – or a 'PT machine' for short.

After all this, and a late, lazy Sunday brunch which she thought would never come to an end, Sophia was almost beside herself with impatience to put her theory and experiment into action.

Sophia had decided that, to safely determine whether the object was, in fact, a time- and space-travel machine, she needed to set the various hands to a time and destination from which she could easily get back if anything went wrong. She had therefore resolved, as soon as she had grabbed her go-bag and made sure that it was stocked with sufficient snacks and drinks, to move the object's time and date hands, just very, very slightly back to the day before; and to move the latitude and longitude hands to the coordinates of the sleepy Anglesey hamlet where Betty was visiting her grandma. There was a campsite on the edge of that village where Sophia had stayed a couple of times with her mum, dad, Ted and Tobes; plus she knew the tiny coastal village itself. She had met up with Betty and her family on the beach and in the village on various occasions on several sunny weekends over the past few years. Sophia wasn't sure quite how accurate the ancient object's latitude and longitude hands, and its date hands, could be, but she reckoned that she knew the area well enough to find her way around so long as she landed somewhere within the locality. Plus she could always find her way to Betty's gran's house, and ultimately get home from there, if she discovered that her theories and the object itself could not be relied on.

So, with no small amount of trepidation, and with a thrilling frisson of excitement like nothing she had ever felt before, Sophia, with Toby at her side, crept up to the hidden hidey-hole room. She opened the old safe and, with her hands shaking slightly but her brow set firm, carefully pulled out the mysterious, ancient, clock-like, time-machine-like object.

With trembling fingers and with her heart beating fast and loud, Sophia moved the various hands attached to the object's beautiful mother-of-pearl face to one day earlier in 2021; Night; 53.3523 in between N and E, 4.2373 W ; and 7 o'clock in the evening...

Chapter 9

Whooshkazzamflashzingwow!!! Sophia experienced a jolt through her body as if she had been struck by lightning. She felt a punch-like thwack in her tummy and her chest, as if all of her breath had been sucked from her for several seconds. She squeezed her eyes tight shut to protect them from the blinding glare of a flashing light that was brighter and more dazzling than anything she had ever seen or suffered before. And then, almost immediately, all was quiet and calm, and Sophia felt absolutely like herself again.

She opened her eyes and was astonished, and ecstatic, to see that she was on the beautiful Anglesey beach that she recognised from all those lovely breakaways with family and friends. The sun was just setting (although it had been around 11 o'clock in the morning just seconds before when she had started her adventure in the hidey-hole room). Sophia knew that she was just a short, coastal walk away from the cosy seaside home where, if her theory was correct, Betty would be visiting her gran, and probably just sitting down to an evening meal, at that very moment.

Sophia took a few moments to take stock of her situation. She was still holding on to the object which, now that it seemed her theory about it being a time- and place- travel machine was correct, and in line with her research, she was referring to as a planisphera-temporalabe – or, a 'PT machine'.

As a serious amateur sleuth and huge fan of Sir Arthur Conan Doyle's detective par excellence Sherlock Holmes, however, Sophia Slewfoot was well aware of the importance of scientific scrutiny and substantiation when it came to anything out of the ordinary or unexplained. Sophia therefore decided not to take anything for granted. Instead, she set out to walk the short, scenic path from the beach round the headland to Betty's gran's cottage, so as to confirm every aspect of her time- and place- travel theory.

Sophia carefully tucked the PT machine into her go-bag and then grabbed her notebook and made a quick record of her experience so far. Sophia precisely logged the jolt, thwack and flash that she had felt after turning the hands of the PT machine; the exact time and date which she had left the hidey-hole room at home; and the apparent time and place at which she now found herself. She noted that the PT machine, which she had been holding on to throughout, had (thankfully!) made the time and place journey to Anglesey with her. Toby, however, whom she had not been holding and who had simply been by her side, had not. She took a few moments to have a quick drink and snack and then made the brief trek round the coastline to where she hoped and expected to see Betty's gran's cottage.

And there it was! And, through the cottage window, there Betty was – with her mum, dad, her brother Reece and her gran. Betty's family were rallying round and all just sitting down to an evening meal of fish, chips and mushy peas. Sophia was happy to see that Betty's grandma was being well-looked after. She was also very happy indeed to verify that both her theory about, and her practical experiment with, the PT machine had been successful. She had set the PT machine's various hands to a time, date and place that she wished to visit, and she had been transported to exactly then and there – as if by magic.

Sophia didn't want to disturb Betty and her family if she really didn't need to, so all that remained was for her to double-check and double-test her theory, by moving the PT machine's hands again – this time to try to get back home to the time, place and date which she had left a short while earlier. Bracing herself for the force which she now knew would accompany her time- and space- travel, Sophia moved the hands on the PT machine back to today's (the real today's) date, to 11 o'clock in the morning (Day) and back to her home coordinates.

And, with a Whooshkazzamflashzingwow!!!, Sophia was home, back in the hidden hidey-hole room once again.

Chapter 10

Monday morning was hard. Sophia found it incredibly difficult to get up, washed and dressed, and out of the door in time for school.

Not only had she had the exceptional and actually quite stressful experience of moving house over that particular weekend, but also she had had the extraordinary, astonishing and electrifying experience of discovering, in an ancient safe hidden away in a secret room at the top of her new home, a time- and space- travel machine which, she had tested with a scientific experiment and confirmed, could transport Sophia to and from any time and place throughout history and throughout the world. To say that Sophia had had a hectic and over-stimulating weekend, and was experiencing a significant degree of exhaustion as a result, was something of an understatement.

However, as tired as Sophia was, she was also absolutely desperate to share with her best friend Betty Babbington the adventures of the weekend and, in particular, her discovery of the amazing PT machine. Somehow, therefore, Sophia managed to drag herself into the shower and then out to school where, at the first available opportunity, she started to update Betty as to her astounding exploits. Before Sophia could really explain, though, the 9 o'clock bell rang for the start of school. Aaagghhh!! Updating Betty would have to wait.

Soon enough, however, as is so often the way, the familiar routine of the school day kicked in, and Sophia found herself completely engrossed in her lessons. In particular, Sophia quickly became totally absorbed in the Monday afternoon lesson of her favourite subject, history.

On this particular Monday, Sophia's history teacher, Mrs Taelim, brought their 'official' lesson (about the Ancient Greeks) to an end slightly early. On so doing, she announced that, for the rest of the week, they were going to supplement their curriculum-dictated history lessons with an independent research project about a fascinating subject – history's mysteries.

Mrs Taelim explained that, throughout history, and despite incredible advances in science, geography and historical record-keeping over time, there have been very many incidents and happenings which remain – even to this day – unexplained. Without going into any detail (this was to be a research project for the pupils after all), Mrs Taelim gave a few headline examples, including the Loch Ness Monster, the Bermuda Triangle, the princes in the Tower, and more. She instructed Sophia and her classmates to use the school and village libraries and the internet to learn about some of history's unsolved mysteries and to write up their findings. The class would then be asked, in a week's time, to share the results of their research about strange happenings and baffling events, in what would no doubt be a fascinating 'show and tell' session.

Well, Sophia was hooked! She found history to be hugely interesting anyway – honestly, you couldn't make up stories that contained more action, adventure, murder, gore and greed than the history of the British monarchy or the Roman Empire, for example – but the idea of researching some of history's unexplained events was something else! The project would combine Sophia's immense interest in history with her absolute passion for investigation and amateur sleuthing! Just imagine, she thought to herself, if I actually managed to solve one of history's mysteries!

Chapter 11

After school that day, Sophia called in to the village library to browse some history books and to speak to the librarians. She wanted to settle upon which history mystery she would study, as she was keen to get started right away.

"Oooh, that sounds like an enjoyable project, Sophia" exclaimed one of the librarians – a young, friendly lady with crazy multi-coloured glasses whose ID badge revealed that she was named 'Miss Reading'. (When Sophia had first met Miss Reading she had thought that, with a name like that, it was perhaps inevitable that Miss Reading had become a librarian, but she was a little disappointed to learn, some time later, that it was actually pronounced 'Redding'!)

"Yes," agreed Sophia, "but I need to decide which mystery to choose before I can really get going."

"Hmm," murmured Miss Reading thoughtfully. "I was always rather fascinated by the mystery of the Marie Celeste – or was it the Mary Celeste? – and the unexplained disappearance of her crew. It's been a while since I read anything about the ship but I remember there were all sorts of theories – ghosts, pirates, sea monsters, magic..."

"Ghosts, pirates, sea monsters, magic??!!" As Sophia repeated Miss Reading's words she knew that she had found the subject of her project. She raced towards the bookshelves and, after just a short while and a little help from Miss Reading, Sophia left the library and walked home, carrying all the books mentioning the mystery of the famous 'ghost' ship that she could find.

Sophia was always starving when she arrived home at the end of the school day, and today was no exception. After pausing only to tell her mum about the exciting project over a typical mid-week tea of fish fingers, chips and peas (with LOADS of ketchup), Sophia settled down in her bedroom, with her library books, the family's tablet, a notebook and pen, and (of course) Toby nestled neatly in her lap. She began her research.

Sophia made notes on some of the key findings she discovered:

- Mary Celeste — American ship found abandoned in the Atlantic Ocean in December 1872.

- Often incorrectly referred to as the 'Marie' Celeste since Arthur Conan Doyle (author of Sherlock Holmes books) wrote a short story[1] based on the mystery, but misspelled the name of the ship!

- The ship had undertaken several previous voyages, but had long suffered bad luck — run aground, caught fire, gone through multiple captains and crews, been associated with financial hardship and several deaths.

- After earlier difficulties and disasters, the Mary Celeste was salvaged and, on 5 November 1872, set sail from New York, bound for Italy. On board were Captain Benjamin Spooner Briggs, his wife and daughter, and a seven-man crew.

- On 5 December 1872, just one month later, a British ship (the Dei Gratia) discovered the Mary Celeste adrift and abandoned. The ship was in excellent, sea-worthy condition, it had plenty of food, drink and other supplies on board, but the captain, his family and the crew were never seen again.

- Navigational equipment and other emergency essentials were missing from the adrift vessel, suggesting that the captain and crew had deliberately departed the ship, despite being in the middle of the ocean, miles and miles from the nearest land (the Azores).

---

1   *J Habakuk Jephson's Statement, Arthur Conan Doyle, 1884*

- What could have happened? Theories:
    a. Piracy (but the ship's cargo was left intact – surely pirates would have looted all treasure?)?
    b. Ghosts, perhaps of former crew members who had died, appearing to the crew and terrifying them into abandoning ship?
    c. Sea monster (kraken, giant squid?)?
    d. Alien abduction?
    e. Bermuda triangle?
    f. Did the crew of the Dei Gratia actually murder and dispose of the crew of the Mary Celeste so that they could heroically 'discover' the ghost ship and reap the salvage reward[2]?
    g. Was there some kind of geographical event or natural disaster that prompted the crew to desert the vessel?
- Most likely theory: an under-sea earthquake caused an unusual wave (or, tsunami) on the surface of the ocean. The captain and crew had not experienced a tsunami before and were so alarmed at the sight of an enormous wave heading towards them, which seemed to appear out of nowhere, that they panicked and abandoned ship – only then to perish at sea. Most likely of all existing theories, but with no records or witnesses to verify this potential account, even this remains pure conjecture and the mystery remains unsolved.

---

2   *Maritime law states that any person or crew who helps to rescue or recover a ship or cargo in peril at sea is entitled to a reward.*

"Wow" thought Sophia. "What an intriguing story." Sophia knew that she had learned enough about the mystery of the Mary Celeste to create a fascinating presentation for her class. She was also very pleased to note that the author of her favourite Sherlock Holmes stories had written about the Mary Celeste mystery and she made a mental note to ask Miss Reading to track down that story for her when she next visited the library! But, oh! How frustrating that she would never actually know the truth of what had really happened!

Or would she...?

Chapter 12

Sophia was torn. She desperately wanted to tell Betty about the PT machine and her experimental adventure with the time- and space- travel trip to Anglesey, and she really wanted to show the secret hidey-hole room and the PT machine to Betty, so that they could experience an adventure together. However, she was now also captivated by the mystery of the Mary Celeste. The possibility had dawned on Sophia that the means to actually answering the enduring question of why the captain, his wife, daughter and crew had abandoned a well-supplied and sea-worthy vessel to surely perish in the middle of the Atlantic Ocean back in Victorian times, was within her grasp.

The mystery had taunted and tantalized people the world over for nearly 150 years, and had given rise to all sorts of wild and wonderful theories. Yet, Sophia's discovery of the mind-boggling PT machine meant that it was now conceivable – even feasible – that she, a ten year old girl from a small, ordinary village in the North of England, might be able to finally explain an enigma that had baffled the world for over a century.

The temptation was too great. It was decided. Sophia would, at the first available opportunity, use her sleuthing skills and the PT machine to visit the time and place of the abandonment of the ghost ship Mary Celeste. She would endeavour to become the first and only person to solve this puzzle – one of history's greatest mysteries of all time!

Chapter 13

Having researched the mystery of the Mary Celeste for her school project on history's mysteries, Sophia had determined upon using the recently discovered PT machine to travel through time and space to the date and location of the apparent abandonment of the world-famous Victorian ghost ship.

Unfortunately, in all the excitement of reading her library books and undertaking internet research to find out all about the fascinating story of the drifting ship and her disappeared crew, Sophia had not noticed that hours had flown by and it was actually now way past her bedtime.

Whilst the PT machine could, as Sophia had discovered, alter time and space to allow a person to travel back into the past and forward into the future, without time in the present seeming to move on at all, nothing could alter the fact that Sophia had been awake, and in a high state of concentration and excitement all day long and, now, into the night. In fact, Sophia realised, she was exhausted. She was also sensible enough to realise that, no matter how eager she might be to put her history-mystery-solving idea into action, it would be foolish, and possibly even dangerous, to take any steps towards the very significant time- and space- travel that this scheme would entail, without both a good night's sleep and some very careful preparation. Calling to mind some of her favourite fictional detectives, she took heed from the fact that one characteristic that Marple, Poirot, Drew, Watson (and, for the most part, Holmes) and Wong (and sometimes Wells) had in common was circumspection. That is, the ability to think carefully and take one's time, to be prudent and plan and, crucially, not to rush too hastily (and therefore carelessly and recklessly) into action.

Sophia therefore resolved to have a good sleep that night, so as to properly rest her 'little grey cells'. She would then formulate a thoughtful and thorough plan the next evening, and set out on her time- and place- travel adventure only when she was really ready.

With that in mind, Sophia changed into her pjs, brushed her teeth, kissed her little brother and her mum and dad goodnight and clambered into bed. Tobes was curled up cosily in his bed at the foot of Sophia's and he panted happily when she whispered to him that they were soon to embark on a great journey of historical exploration.

Almost immediately, Sophia drifted into a deep sleep. Her dreams that night were filled with oceans and adventures, ghosts and pirates, krakens and crooks... Floating through them all, on an ethereal sailing ship, battling spectral winds and towering, unexplained waves, with Tobes at her feet and the mystical PT machine clutched tightly in her hands, was our brave, time-travelling sleuth, Sophia...

Chapter 14

Sophia woke early the next morning. Although she had slept and felt rested, her brain had been working through her dreams and she had actually all-but formed her plan.

On three days each week Sophia's mum and dad both worked, and Sophia and Ted went to 'After School Club', where they played with their friends and ate copious amounts of fruit and snacks (healthy, of course), until one of their parents could finish work and collect them. However, Sophia's mum never worked on Tuesdays, and so Sophia was always home on Tuesdays by shortly after 3.30 in the afternoon. That particular Tuesday, Sophia had plenty of time to get home, get changed, have a snack, and have a quick chat with her mum about her day, before finalising her plan for travelling through time and space to solve the mystery of the Mary Celeste.

Apart from the fact that Sophia didn't want her family to suspect that anything out of the ordinary was afoot, Sophia's Tuesday afternoon catch-up with her mum was one of her favourite times of every week. On other days it was a bit of a rush, after After

School Club, to get home, play with Tobes, do any homework, practise any spellings, get fed, bathed, changed and into her room by bedtime. Tuesday afternoons, however, seemed to stretch out before Sophia, especially when the nights began to get lighter as spring moved towards summer, as it was just beginning to do. She relished the extra time spent with her mum, Toby and even (on occasion, when he wasn't doing Lego, practising keepy-uppies or annoying her in some way as little brothers often do) Ted.

That day, after chatting happily with her mum about what she had learned in school; with whom she and Betty had played; what they had played at break times; what she had had for lunch; and so on, Sophia pocketed a bag of Toby's favourite chewy chicken treats from the dog box in the kitchen, and made her way upstairs. She was determined to hold on tightly to Toby so that he came with her on the adventure this time and she wanted to ensure that, if he felt at all agitated or unhappy, she had a treat to hand to calm and settle him at any time. Then, with the blissfully unaware Tobes trotting merrily at her feet, Sophia grabbed her go-bag and... it was go time!

Chapter 15

Up in the hidey-hole room at the top of the secret, circular stairwell, behind the hidden door on the landing of her new home, Sophia turned the ornate key in the lock of the old safe and brought out the marvellous PT machine.

With her go-bag on her back and Toby tucked tightly under her left arm, Sophia reached out with her right arm and slowly, carefully, began to move the various hands across the shimmering mother-of-pearl face.

As part of her planning, Sophia had decided to set the date for 3 December 1872, just a few days before the 'ghost ship' Mary Celeste had been discovered by the rescue ship, the Dei Gratia. Although nobody knew the exact date on which the crew had abandoned ship, Sophia deduced, from accounts which described the fairly immaculate state in which the Mary Celeste had been found, that not very much time at all must have elapsed between the abandonment and the discovery.

Thanks to maritime records about the location in which the Mary Celeste had been found, made public in the huge amount of press and literature surrounding the mystery, Sophia was able to set quite accurate latitude and longitude co-ordinates on the PT machine.

She had no idea what time of day or night would give her the best chance of witnessing what had happened on the fateful date and so, for want of any better ideas, she left the Day/Night and time hands in their existing position, reflecting the current time of day in the here and now – around 5 o'clock in the afternoon...

Suddenly, and with a

w h o o s h k a z z a m f l a s h z i n g wow!!!, Sophia and a very surprised and slightly distressed Toby found themselves on the quiet and empty deck of a huge Victorian sailing ship, floating peacefully in a cold, calm ocean. The sun had obviously set only recently and the sky had the ghostly half-light of a winter evening's dusk.

Toby was whimpering quietly and cuddling up to Sophia for comfort and reassurance. Sophia fed him a few treats, which seemed to help but, to be honest, she was quite glad to feel the warmth and familiarity of Toby close to her too.

On one hand, Sophia felt slightly disappointed because the ship seemed so quiet that she wondered whether she had set the PT machine to a date that was too late, and that she had already missed whatever had happened to the Mary Celeste's crew. On the other, however, and despite the eerie emptiness of the ship's deck, Sophia had the disquieting sense that she and Tobes were not alone. It was time to investigate.

Putting the PT machine safely into her go-bag – it was, after all, her one-and-only lifeline back to the present day and to her home and family – Sophia whispered to Toby that all was ok, but that they were going to explore the ship. Sophia gently stroked Toby and told him that there was nothing to worry about, but that he should stay very quiet and calm, just in case.

As always, Toby seemed to understand exactly what Sophia was saying to him, and he padded next to her, without making a sound, as she started to thoroughly and methodically survey the situation.

Sophia took stock. She decided that the phrase 'ghost ship' was very apt indeed. In the still waters of the mid-Atlantic on a serene but cool winter's evening, the deathly quiet ship bobbed and rolled gently, making Sophia feel as if she herself were floating, spirit-like and insubstantial. For a few moments, Sophia focused on the strangeness of the setting – the unfamiliar sights, sounds and smells of the sea. The magical distortion of time and space that had brought Sophia to this place all added to an unnatural, other-worldly atmosphere that Sophia knew she would struggle to describe. She could feel it though – as real as a pinch – a sense of forboding that crept, like a chill, right through her body and into her very bones. Toby felt it too. He was silent and watchful and his fur stood on end all along his spine. He seemed to go tense, and on the alert, every time a lone sea bird cawed or cried into the night, and every time a shifting, wispy cloud drifted, like a spectre, across the surface of the sea beside them and up into the darkening sky above.

Shaking off unsettling thoughts about ghostly spirits, Sophia discovered quickly that there was little to be learned from the quiet, empty, clean and clear deck. At the far end, however, Sophia could just make out what appeared to be some steps – presumably leading down into the ship's hull. Sophia guessed that, if the captain, his family and the crew, were still on ship, they might be below deck at this time in the evening. It was definitely getting chillier and darker by the minute and Sophia reasoned that, after a hard day's sailing, the crew would probably, by now, be enjoying their evening meal before retiring to their living and sleeping quarters for the night.

Sophia was right! As she and Tobes crept carefully and quietly down the stairs, she began to hear the muffled sound of voices. Sophia had studied several pictures of the Mary Celeste before setting off on her adventure, so she had a pretty good idea of the layout of the ship. She was therefore able to work out that the voices were coming from the captain's cabin.

Chapter 16

Sophia and Toby made their way towards the captain's cabin. As they grew closer, the voices that they could hear became louder and less muffled. Sophia saw that there was a small cupboard-like nook just a little way away from the closed door to the cabin. The nook was enclosed by a rich-looking, red velvet curtain, and contained a few brooms, buckets, cloths and other light cleaning paraphernalia. It would make the perfect place to hide and listen! Sophia sat down on an overturned bucket and lifted Toby into her lap. Shivering a little – partly with excitement and partly because of the chill in the December evening air – Sophia arranged the velvet curtain across the nook so that she and Tobes couldn't be seen, but so that the voices coming from inside the captain's cabin could be clearly heard.

"Well, beggar my beliefs Capt'n! I never knowed this ship had had so much bad luck or I'd never have agreed to serve on her!" said one voice, sharply and with a tremble of what sounded like fear.

"Don't be so superstitious!" jeered another voice. "Most of the ships in this ocean have had the odd blaze or grounding at some point, and you know the saying's true: there's worse things happen at sea."

"Aye," added a third voice, with a touch of drama, "there's stories I could tell ye about sailors from across the seven seas perishing in the jaws of sea monsters, being carried off into the heavens in the claws of colossal bird-beasts, being torn from top to toe by marauding pirates..."

"Aah, but those are just stories, m'lad. If ye all really want te feel the heebie-jeebies, let me tell you about all those poor souls who perished on this very ship, oh yea, and haunt it to this day, so they do. First, there's old Capt'n McLellan. He got sick and died sudden-like, just a few short days after settin' foot aboard this vessel. Then there's all them fellas who drowned in the Channel crash just a little while later in '61; and them that passed in the winds and the waves, the storm and the swells off Cap' Breton in '67... I'm tellin' ye – I've heard the screams and moans, and felt the spirits and the terror, of all them poor mates every single night I've been aboard this 'ere keel..."

Sophia felt the hairs on the back of her neck stand up and an icy chill flow through her as she listened to this last voice. The words were spoken quietly, and creepily, and were met with hushed silence by all those present in the captain's cabin.

The captain and crew of the Mary Celeste had obviously been passing the long hours of an evening at sea telling tales of the ship's tragedies suffered in times gone by. Just like when Sophia had experienced the spine-tingling fun of telling (not too-scary) ghost stories on Halloween, the sailors had been regaling each other with tall tales of monstrous creatures and unfortunate events. However, even from her hiding place in the nook outside the cabin, Sophia could feel the mood change, and a frightened chill flow through the air, when this last old mate spoke of the tortured ghosts of perished past ship-mates roaming the vessel on a never-ending nightly basis...

It was amongst this fraught and frightened atmosphere that, abruptly and apparently out of nowhere, a huge tremor suddenly trembled and shook the boat. It seemed to Sophia as though, from the bowels of the earth, an unexplained blast of force had violently exploded and had caused the ship to shudder and judder in an unearthly and unnatural manner. It was as if, Sophia thought, the ship itself was quaking in fear of some unknown and misunderstood terror.

Sophia knew, from the research that she had undertaken prior to this adventure, that what she and the crew members had just felt was, in all likelihood, an undersea earthquake. Sophia had studied earthquakes in her geography lessons at school. She knew that, just like the causes of earthquakes that occurred across the world on land, the movement of the earth's tectonic plates and changes in pressure along fault lines under the sea could often result in quite significant undersea quakes.

Sophia couldn't see the ocean from where she and Tobes were hiding, but she also knew that undersea earthquakes often caused huge giant waves, known as tsunamis. Tsunamis could reach towering heights – sometimes of over 100 feet – and could speed across the surface of the sea at up to 500 miles per hour. Sophia could well imagine that, if the captain and crew of the Mary Celeste had seen, from the cabin's windows, an awe-inspiring, massive swell rise up and race across the ocean under a darkening December sky, whilst experiencing the violent blast and buffeting that the boat was continuing to suffer, that would indeed induce feelings of shock, horror and anxiety in the extreme amongst the Victorian crew and its captain.

Sophia quickly cuddled Toby even closer to her. She stroked and soothed him and offered reassurance that she wasn't sure she really felt herself. The two of them cowered together in their nook, with brooms and brushes and buckets falling and crashing all around them, waiting and hoping for the terrible trembling and shuddering to cease.

Chapter 17

And cease it soon did. Almost as suddenly as the blast beneath the boat and its repercussions on board had been felt, a cool and almost eerie calm settled across the ocean, causing the ship to merely loll and roll gently, floating serenely on the sea's surface once again.

What was not calm, however, was the commotion coming from the captain's cabin. As Sophia and Toby crouched in their nook they heard the door to the captain's cabin being flung open and crew members running wild. Sophia decided to take a calculated risk. She reckoned that she could afford, amidst the pandemonium, to safely sneak a peek past the curtain.

The crew were plainly frightened out of their wits. Amongst the mêlée of the seven crew members that Sophia counted running, screaming and screeching, in all directions from the cabin, there was also a more richly dressed man, who was clearly Captain Briggs. The captain was calling out urgent instructions: to his wife to grab their daughter; and to his crew to ready the yawl. He yelled, at the top of his booming voice so that all could hear him, that they were immediately to abandon ship before the terrible ghouls of ship-mates past swelled the seas once more and dragged them to their own watery graves!

Chapter 18

So that was it! Sophia now knew – as did no other person on the planet, from the date of 3 December 1872 through over 150 years of history to the real life present day – the real reason behind the mystery of the Mary Celeste.

The ship's captain and crew, already worked up into a state of fear and fright following their tales of disasters, drownings and hauntings on board, had sprung into a state of high panic when the Mary Celeste had been battered and shaken by an undersea earthquake. While she (unfortunately?!) had not witnessed the sight of a swell herself, Sophia deduced from the sailors' panicked cries that they had also seen a tsunami racing across the ocean, and that Captain Briggs had therefore made the snap decision to abandon ship. Sophia understood that he was counting on taking action – fleeing in a desperate effort to survive and to save his family and crew – rather than doing nothing, and risking the ship being smashed and sunk if the great wave were to envelop the vessel.

And then it dawned on Sophia – she was actually

in a terrible dilemma. If she stayed quiet and hidden, and simply used the PT machine to whisk her and Toby back to the safety of the hidey-hole room at home in the real life present day, Captain Briggs, his wife, their two year old daughter, and the seven crew members would all perish at sea, never to be seen again...

However, if she spoke up and tried to save them, explaining, with the benefit of her knowledge of the future, that the boat would weather the incident unscathed, with not even a scratch on her immaculately swept deck, or a tear in any of her fine, white sails, then what would happen?! The crew might assume she was a mad stowaway or a wicked sea-witch (Sophia knew that Victorian sailors were notorious for their superstitions when away at sea), and they might harm or imprison her and Tobes. Even worse, they might separate them from the PT machine, leaving Sophia and Toby trapped for ever more in 1872 and subject to the same terrible fate that she knew otherwise awaited the crew of the Mary Celeste.

Even in the unlikely event that the petrified and unwitting crew did believe that a ten year old girl and her dog from the future could save them from the perils of an unfamiliar and unnatural (or so they thought) disaster, Sophia realised, as any time-traveller must, that anything at all that she did to interact with the crew – indeed any action taken by her at all that had even the smallest impact or effect on any other person or event – would alter the course of history forever. If she did manage to convince the captain and the crew not to abandon ship and to ride out the quake and any swell, then the mystery of the Mary Celeste would never even arise. History books, newspapers and internet pages throughout the next/last 150 years would be wiped clean of any mention of the enigma; and journalists, historical sleuths and mystery-lovers across the world would have to find another story with which to concern themselves.

Sophia realised that she was experiencing what the 1985 film 'Back to the Future'[3] had explored: the paradox that any action by a time-traveller in the past could cause untold ripple effects which could potentially result in their purpose for time-travelling, or even the time-traveller him- or herself, not to exist.

Aggghhhh!!! What on earth should Sophia do?!

---

[3]   *A Steven Spielberg film. Written by Robert Zemeckis and Bob Gale, directed by Zemeckis.*

Chapter 19

Sophia was in an impossible position. Should she reveal herself and Tobes to the fear-crazed crew of the Mary Celeste and try to save them, endangering herself, Toby and potentially all future-history, in so doing? Or should she simply re-set the hands of the PT machine to the safety of her home and the present day and literally abandon the ship herself?

Sophia desperately wanted to be circumspect, to think things through carefully and do all that she could to reach the right decision, but, ironically, the choices she was facing were not ones which much more time would be likely to resolve in any event. No matter how long Sophia agonized over her decision, and even if she used the PT machine to buy herself more time to think, the reaction of the crew to the appearance of a small girl and her dog from the future, espousing a

jargon-filled scientific explanation of plate tectonics and oceanology as to why they should remain on the ship and ride out the undersea quake, was always going to risk a hugely unfavourable reaction.

Whatever happened though, Sophia reasoned, the absolute most important issue was that Sophia, Tobes and the PT machine must not, on any account become separated. Sophia therefore unbuckled the belt from her jeans and looped it through, not only her own belt hooks, but also Toby's collar and the handle at the top of the PT machine. It was very uncomfortable – for Toby to find his head suddenly jammed up tightly against Sophia's waist; and for Sophia to have the PT machine banging awkwardly against her thigh every time she moved – but it was entirely necessary.

With that done, Sophia took a deep breath and leapt out from behind the red curtain, very much to the surprise of Captain Briggs, who had gathered various essential navigation equipment into his arms and was racing towards where the yawl was about to be released from the deck.

Luckily for Sophia, the sight of a small girl, attached to a dog and to a strange-looking clock-like machine, and wearing jeans (a girl wearing trousers?!) and a t-shirt (a t-shirt?!)[4], stunned Captain Briggs into silence and inaction. Sophia took advantage. She immediately and concisely explained, pointing to the PT machine, that she had arrived from the future to share both her knowledge of undersea earthquakes and consequential swells and also her absolute certainty that the Mary Celeste would survive the current incident unscathed.

Sophia quickly pulled her notebook out of her go-bag. She showed the key points from her research to the gobsmacked captain and begged him to re-consider his panicked and hasty decision to abandon ship so far from any shore. Then, before he had time to argue or indeed even to react in any way, Sophia re-set the hands of the PT machine to her home time and place and, with a whooshkazzamflashzingwow!!!, disappeared before his very eyes.

---

4 *Jeans and a t-shirt, never mind on a girl, would probably have been unseen and unheard of in 1872.*

Chapter 20

And that was it! Before they knew it, Sophia and Toby were safely back in the hidey-hole room at the top of the house once again. Toby wasn't particularly unsettled by the jolt, thwack and flash of his journey through time and space now that he had experienced it a second time, but he snuffled against Sophia to beg for a treat anyway. Sophia, elated with the success of her history mystery-solving adventure and her safe return home, was only too happy to oblige.

Sophia felt on an absolute high! She had actually travelled through time and space to the date on which the crew of the Mary Celeste had decided to abandon ship, and so now she knew the answer to a mystery that had baffled countless minds throughout history and even to the present day! She had put to great use her love of history, research, discovery and exploration and her passion for mysteries and amateur sleuthing! It was an amazing feeling.

Sophia wished that she could tell her family about the PT machine and her remarkable adventure, but she knew that, despite her safe return home, her mum and dad would be horrified, terrified even, at the risks that Sophia had taken in using the PT machine. She felt sure that they would confiscate the machine and ban her from time-travelling for life. She resigned herself to the fact that she would have to keep her fantastic exploits a secret from her family. Sophia knew, though, that Betty could definitely be trusted to keep the secret, and so she would content herself with telling Betty everything in due course.

In the meantime, Sophia decided to nip downstairs and give her mum a quick hug. After all, alongside feelings of elation, Sophia was also more than a little relieved to be home, safe and sound, after such a daring and potentially perilous adventure. She also wanted to check, via the internet, the impact of her endeavours on the fate of the crew of the Mary Celeste.

Sophia's mum was touched to suddenly receive an unexpected and unprompted cuddle from her ten year old daughter, but soon put it down to inevitable pre-teen tactics when Sophia subsequently requested an additional twenty minutes on the tablet, even though all of her homework for that day had been done.

Rolling her eyes and laughing, Sophia's mum handed over the tablet. Sophia raced up to her room, where Toby had already settled himself happily back into his own bed, and typed "Mary Celeste mystery" into the search engine right away.

There was nothing. Sophia could find no mention, anywhere, of any mystery surrounding the Victorian vessel known as the Mary Celeste. Next, Sophia typed in "Mary Celeste ghost ship" and "Mary Celeste crew disappearance" but, again and again, no items or articles of any interest appeared.

The only information about the Mary Celeste which Sophia could find anywhere on the internet was bland and factual, noting the names of her several captains and the dates and purposes of her various, and generally, successful, commercial voyages. Sophia did find references to a collision which the ship had endured in the English Channel in 1861, and to a storm in which it received some damage off Cape Breton in 1867, but that was pretty much it.

Sophia turned to the history books that she had borrowed from the library. She discovered, to her amazement, that all of the chapters and references to the Mary Celeste that she had seen in the books and read before, had simply disappeared.

Finally, just as she was about to give up her research, Sophia eventually found one small reference, in a dry academic internet article about vessels involved in international trade in Victorian times, to the fact that the Mary Celeste had successfully transported its cargo from New York to Italy, in late 1872 and early 1873, without incident.

"We did it, Tobes!" cried Sophia ecstatically. "We saved the crew of the Mary Celeste! Nobody else will ever know of the mystery that we solved and the lives that we saved, but we know, Toby, we know!"

Sophia gave Toby a lovely long cuddle before getting ready for bed herself and settling down to drift off to sleep while enjoyably musing over the excitement and satisfaction of her amazing time- and space-travelling adventure, and her solution to one of history's greatest mysteries of all time. And then it dawned on her...

...The time travel ripple effect! It had rendered the mystery of the Mary Celeste – and therefore her school project – a complete nonsense! The story of the Mary Celeste and its disappearing crew had now never actually happened! "Aah, Tobes!" laughed Sophia. "I'll have to choose another history mystery now... and start my project all over again!"

✳ ✳ ✳

If you have enjoyed this book, please visit **www.sophiaslewfoot.co.uk** to find out more!

From the website you can sign up to receive news and notifications of forthcoming Sophia Slewfoot Solves History's Mysteries books and you can follow Sophia Slewfoot on social media (Twitter @SSlewfoot; Instagram sophiaslewfoot).

Coming soon

History fan Sophia Slewfoot is a budding amateur detective who loves nothing more than curling up with a good whodunnit or, even better, finding a real life mystery to unravel. Join Sophia, her best friend Betty and her beloved Beagle Toby, as they embark on amazing adventures to solve some of the many mysteries which, throughout history and even to this day, have otherwise remained unexplained...

The Mystery of the Oak Island Treasure

What is the mystery of the Oak Island Treasure? Is it true that pirate treasure lays buried in a pit on the infamous Oak Island, and that a curse follows all who seek it? Can Sophia and Betty solve the mystery that has confounded some of the world's most committed treasure hunters over the last few hundred years? Can they even find (and recover?!) the fabled priceless treasure?! Delve into myth, legend, fact and more than a little fiction, to accompany Sophia and Betty on a nerve-wracking, nail-biting, history's mystery-solving mission.

Shergar the Stolen Stallion

Sophia and her best friend Betty Babbington have found themselves embroiled in a shocking mystery which combines their love of history with their passion for all things horse riding-related.

What happened to Shergar? How did he disappear, as if into thin air? Can Sophia and Betty solve the mystery that rocked the racing world and baffled the police, international investigators and the world's media? Can they even discover (and rescue?!) the magnificent racing champion?!

Delve into myth, legend, fact and more than a little fiction, to accompany Sophia and Betty on a fast-paced, perilous history's mystery-solving mission.

S pecial Edition, in association with
Crieff Hydro Hotel & Resort:

Crieff Hydro's White Lady

Who was the Crieff Hydro White Lady? Where did she come from? When did she come from? Was she good or was she evil? Does she still roam the hotel?!

Delve into myth, legend, fact and more than a little fiction, to accompany Sophia on a very special, one-off history's mystery-solving mission based at an exceptional, historical, Scottish family resort.

Printed in Great Britain
by Amazon

00058